To Esme, Ellie, Oliver, Grace, Daisy and their mums and dads:
Ben, Jessica, Lucy, Tom, Martin and Lisa.
Great-grandma Shirley's wonderful little brood!

Neil x

Red Robin BOOKS
Where story matters

Red Robin Books is an imprint of Corner To Learn Limited

Published by
Corner To Learn Limited
Willow Cottage • 26 Purton Stoke • Swindon • Wiltshire SN5 4JF • UK
ISBN: 978-1-905434-97-8
First published in the UK 2012
Text © Neil Griffiths 2012
Illustrations © Christine Grove 2012

Design by
David Rose

Printed in China

ESME'S EGG

Neil Griffiths

Illustrated by
Christine Grove

Esme was sitting cosily, as she usually did during the laying season, in her snug nesting box. Perched just above her, Arthur the cockerel noisily welcomed in the morning as he always did, whilst outside some of the hens were already pecking for grubs as they endlessly did.

Beneath Esme, warmed by her fluffy feathers,
nestled one brown and slightly speckled egg.
But as he regularly did, Farmer
Ferguson arrived and, despite
all her angry protests, shooed
Esme from her nest and took
the egg she had
so proudly laid.

"Why," thought Esme, "after all this effort did he always take
her precious egg?" After all, it was HER egg, not HIS!
Esme decided enough was enough and she hatched a plan!

The following day began as it always did. Arthur was in full cry. There was lots of pecking outside. But a determined Esme was in position in her box.

Farmer Ferguson arrived as usual and began to shoo Esme. Esme sat firmly! Today she was not for shooing!

Farmer Ferguson tried again. Still Esme didn't budge.

Tired of shooing, Farmer Ferguson simply lifted a furious Esme up in the air, removed her brown and slightly speckled egg and plopped her unceremoniously back on her nest.

Esme was furious! So she hatched another plan.

The following morning, Arthur was at it again, there was plenty of pecking outside, which goes without saying, but no Esme in her nesting box! Esme had craftily found another spot to lay her egg and was nesting smugly at the back of the barn.

But her smug look was not to last long, as Farmer Ferguson spotted her tail feathers protruding above the bucket. He lifted Esme up and this time, flung her through the barn door.

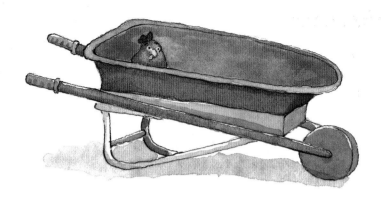

Over the days that followed, Esme did all she
could to outwit the farmer. First it was in a wheelbarrow, then
inside the tractor cab and finally she even braved the lower
branches of an apple tree. But each time, Farmer Ferguson
found her and removed her brown and slightly speckled egg.
Esme returned to her nesting box, ruffled but not beaten.
She had hatched a further cunning plan.

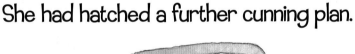

The following morning, there was Arthur's usual
performance, non-stop pecking outside but
unusually there was no Esme, although one brown
and slightly speckled egg did lie in the nesting box.

A surprised Farmer Ferguson took the egg and
set off back to the farmhouse.

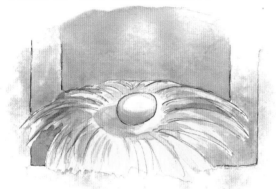

Esme, who had only briefly abandoned the egg and had been
lurking beneath the chicken coup, followed behind him.
She watched as he entered the outhouse at the side of the
farmhouse and then waited in hiding until he came out again.

Once the coast was clear, she entered the shed and, to her surprise, found it was full of eggs on shelves, set out neatly in rows.

But Esme knew her egg anywhere and spotted it instantly in a tray. She fluttered her way onto the shelf and settled down on her beloved egg. There, she sat more determined than ever till the following day.

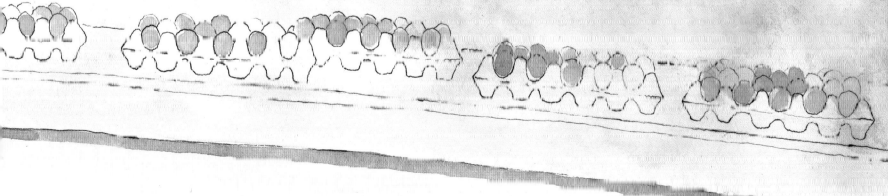

Early next morning, Esme thought what a joy it was not to be woken by Arthur's noisy cockadoodling.

But this peaceful start to the day was soon disturbed by footsteps, so Esme hid hastily.

It was Farmer Ferguson. Esme watched as he carefully lifted the trays and proceeded to carry them out and place them in the back of his old green van.

EGG-123

She knew she couldn't waste a moment. She scuttled at top speed, flapped her wings and gained just enough height to enter the back of the van, narrowly missing the trays of eggs.

Once dusted down, Esme took cover behind a spare tyre as Farmer Ferguson closed the van door.

What followed could only be described as Esme's worst nightmare. It was so dark in the back of the van that she could hardly see which egg was which, but she relied on instinct and finally felt an egg she just knew was hers.

However, the trouble had only just begun. Once Farmer Ferguson started the engine and began to drive off, Esme was thrown from one side of the van to the other. Each time, she frantically scrambled back and repositioned herself over her egg.

After half an hour of bouncing and swerving, the van finally came to an abrupt halt, which hurtled a dizzy and dazed Esme to the floor.

Farmer Ferguson opened the door and Esme watched as he took the trays inside a building that was bigger than any building she had ever seen.

Esme followed cautiously. Once inside, Esme could hardly believe her eyes. There were eggs everywhere! She knew she mustn't take her eyes off her egg. But that wasn't easy! They went up, down, round and round. They were sized, sorted, washed and boxed.

Not once did dear old Esme take her eyes off her brown and slightly speckled egg. She knew exactly which box it was in. She was just about to sit on it, when again it was whisked off and loaded into larger trays in the back of a huge lorry.

With only seconds to spare, Esme hurtled
in and settled on the box that held her egg.
There she sat for several dark but less
bumpy hours. In fact, she even managed
to get a little sleep.

She was woken by the clunking of the lock on the back doors of the lorry. A young man in much smarter clothes than Farmer Ferguson lifted the trays from the lorry and placed them on a trolley.

Esme took her chance and hitched a ride beneath the trays into a large storeroom with tins, boxes and packages of every shape and size.

A young lady took the tray that had Esme's egg box in it through some sliding doors. Esme would now need all the courage she could muster.

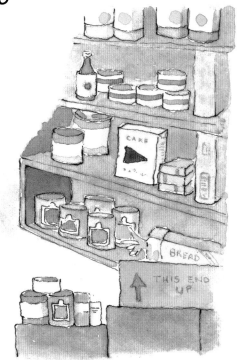

As the doors opened again, she darted from one shelf to another, all the time following the footsteps of the young lady and not taking her eyes off her feet for one moment.

Finally, she stopped and Esme could see her place the box on a high shelf with other boxes nearby. Now Esme faced her biggest challenge. How on earth was she to get up to that high shelf? Chickens are not renowned for flying very well and rarely reached this height.

But Esme was not going to be beaten at this late stage. She would need all the nerve she could muster. She seized her moment as a customer's trolley began to head her way. With one short climb up a tower of tins and then a dainty tip-toe across a moving trolley, followed by a final fling, Esme hurtled onto the shelf. There she dusted herself down and settled on her egg at last. She remained there for several days, disturbed only by the odd removal of boxes that surrounded her.

In fact, Esme began to enjoy her new tranquil surroundings. No noisy Arthur or fussy pecking hens to tolerate. And no Farmer Ferguson disturbing her! Her courageous efforts seemed to be paying off. Well, they were, until a large hand reached to the back of the shelf and grabbed Esme by the neck.

She panicked and pecked at it
violently. What followed can only be
described as pandemonium.
The customer screamed hysterically.
"Help, help! I've been attacked by a
vile creature on the shelf!"
"Vile!" thought Esme. "How dare she?"

An assistant rushed to the customer's aid, but was too scared to look, so she called a supervisor. But she was also too scared. Finally, the manager arrived wearing gloves and gripping a broomstick. He nervously stepped forward and poked the end towards Esme.

Esme hadn't come this far to be prodded off her egg by a broom. She puffed up her feathers, inflated her chest and propelled herself at full speed towards the broom handle, knocking both the manager and what was now a rather large crowd to the floor.
Tins tumbled, boxes bounced and cartons cascaded. A rather dazed manager soon realised that this so-called vile creature was in fact a furious chicken.
Expert help was required!

A short time later, Farmer Ferguson arrived. "Oh no," thought Esme, despairingly. "Not him again!" But her despair was short lived, as she was distracted by a tapping sound coming from beneath her tummy feathers. This was followed by wriggling and squirming. Esme was so mesmerised by this that she didn't notice Farmer Ferguson gently lift her and the egg box from the shelf.

Once cradled safely in his arms, Esme raised herself up from the box. To her astonishment, there beneath her chirped not one but six tiny chicks! "Amazing!" thought Esme. "Simply amazing!"

Nutritional [Information]

Average values	[per] 100g
Energy	[...]27kJ / 151kcal
Protein	12.5g
Carbohydrate	Trace
Fat	11.2g
of which saturates	3.2g
Sodium	0.14g
Salt equivalent	0.35g

Store in a cool dry place.

FARM FRESH 100%

The crowd cheered loudly and Farmer Ferguson
whispered, "Well done, old girl!"
A proud Esme settled back down gently and fluffed
up her feathers again to keep the chicks warm.

Farmer Ferguson placed them gently on the front seat of the van and made his way back home.

Life back at the farm changed very little. Arthur was as noisy as ever. The hens pecked endlessly as they always did. And Farmer Ferguson collected eggs as he usually did. But as you can see, life for Esme had changed forever!

The chicken and the egg!

Tail feathers

Saddle

Back

Comb

Ear

Eye

Beak

Nostril

Neck

Shoulder

Breast

Wing

Contour feathers
cover the body

Thigh

Hock

Shank

Ankle

Chickens originated from South-East Asia but due to the migration of people, over a long period of time, can now be found all over the world.

In the UK, adult male chickens are called *cocks*, whereas in North America they are called *roosters*. Males under a year old are *cockerels*. Females over a year old are known as *hens*, and younger females are *pullets*. A general term used for a chicken is *chook*. Babies are called *chicks*.

There are two types of chicken - pure breeds and hybrids. Pure breeds have been specifically bred to show certain traits and features. A hybrid is a typical brown hen, like Esme, which has been especially bred to be a robust bird and a good egg-layer.

It is estimated that at any one moment there are approximately 20 billion chickens in the world!

Chickens will eat most things, but domestic animals are fed whole wheat, grit and special pellets containing all the essential nutrients and vitamins they require.

Free range is a term which means that the chickens have been allowed to roam freely instead of being contained in any manner.

Eggs are oval in shape, allowing them to roll in a circular direction, but meaning they will never roll far from the nest.

Egg colour is normally related to the colour of the chickens' ears - red ears produce brown eggs, white ears produce white eggs.

Depending on the breed of hen, it may lay a few eggs over many years or a lot of eggs over a few years.

29 million eggs a day are consumed in the UK.

The colour of egg yolk will be a deeper yellow if the chickens eat more grass.

Bad eggs float!

Eggs make a great meal and are full of nutrients and protein. They can be boiled, poached, fried, scrambled or make a great omelette.

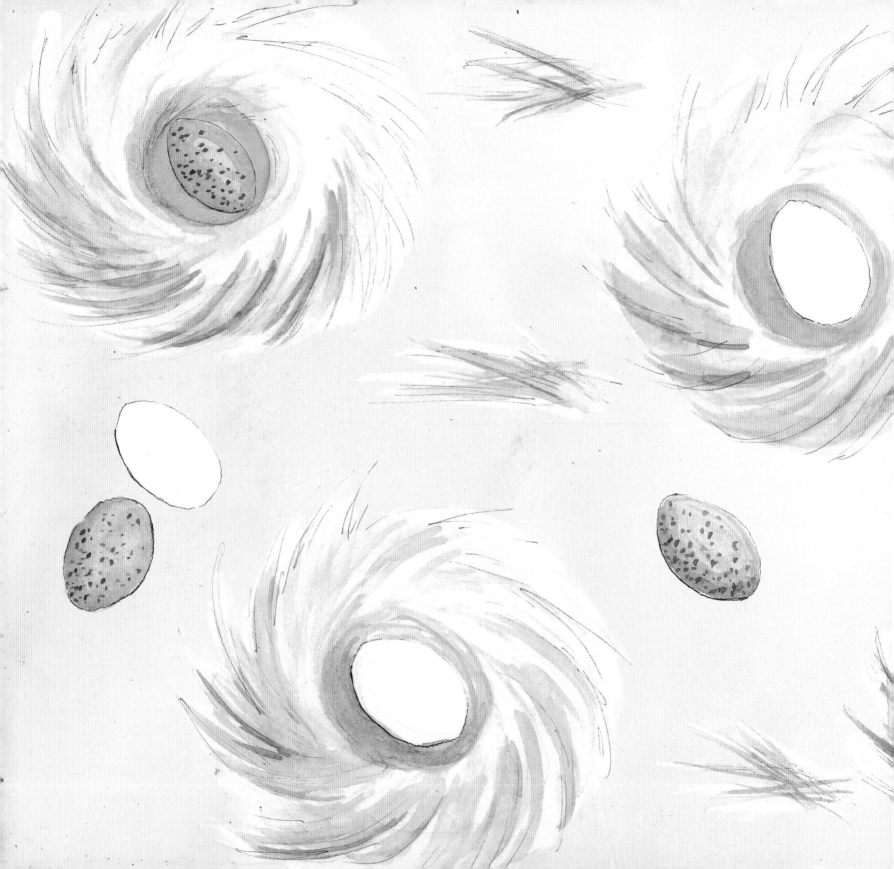